AQUARIANS AND ACQUISITIONS

AQUARIANS AND ACQUISITIONS

LEIGH MARIS

Splintered Orchard Press

Aquarians and Acquisitions
by Leigh Maris

Copyright © 2024 Leigh Maris

Paperback ISBN: 979-8-9899667-0-7
eBook ISBN: 979-8-9899667-1-4

First paperback and eBook edition published on February 29, 2024.

Splintered Orchard Press an Imprint of Splintered Orchard Press LLC

splinteredorchardpress.com

Aquarians and Acquisitions

Len Rivers stands in his kitchen in front of a paper calendar that is secured to the lime green wall in front of him by a single grey thumbtack. An image of clean, royal blue water and vibrant town houses all stacked atop each other lays on the upper most page of his calendar. Across the top of the lower most page are the month and year: APRIL 2063. Several boxes fill the negative space below the month and year.

Len lifts his left hand to the page. The fine, red tip of a permanent marker protrudes from his grip. He holds the permanent marker flush to the box on his calendar marked "17." Slowly and methodically, he circles this seventeenth box three times. Len has waited ten years for this day.

He glances toward his living room, which is teeming with conversation he can only make out in bits over the distance. Before Len tears himself away from the kitchen to join the muffled voices he overhears, he glances back at his calendar. He strikes through days one through sixteen of April 2063 frantically. Len has a known habit of forgetting the day because he is too focused on the future.

Except now the future has come.

Around him, the whole globe hums. April 17, 2063. The whole globe has been waiting ten years for this day. Not just Len.

Today is the day that the seven scientists of varying disciplines, including marine biology and physics, six astronauts, four engineers, four global security analysts, two diplomats, and one information technologist that the World Habitability Project deployed on the world's first manned mission to Inundo return to Earth. The mission to Inundo, Earth's neighboring water-giant, spanned ten years in whole. Some journalists fancy calling the quest Mission Habitable Status. Eight of those years were travel alone: four years to Inundo and four years back to Earth. The distance traveled was 317,100 AU round trip. Two of those ten years in mission were spent actually on the Earth's neighboring water-giant.

The media has been reporting on this date for weeks. Now that the day has dawned, Len sees notifications from *Science 4 Tomorrow* and *The Other Frontier* flood the screen in the upper left side of his eyeglasses.

The notifications of the WHP Space Team's return to Earth reminds Len of the original media coverage clipped to the corkboard above his desk. He can see the layout of the media feature in his eidetic memory. An image splays across the page of the large crew of twenty-four people as they step into three large spacecraft while wearing helmets that look unusually like fishbowls. Patched onto the upper right arms of their spacesuits is a Mission Habitable Status insignia. The design of the insignia is an anchor with a small goldfish in the foreground. Around the image of the crew is little black text summarizing the mission the crew would embark upon and a few short interviews with crew members. One of those crew members was May Rivers, Len's little sister.

Len pinned that clipping above his desk in 2054 and has kept it there ever since. He treasured the clipping for more reasons than his little sister's feature, although he would be lying if he said he wasn't proud of her and a little envious, too. Years into the mission, he saw no reason to take it down. In fact, being a member of the scientific community, seeing that clipping of the people who signed up to save the future of humanity focuses Len on what matters. Whenever he is assigned a new project, which often does not meet the WHP protocol for new infrastructure developments, he remembers why the WHP protocol is so important.

Seeing that clipping above his desk lets him imagine a future Earth with structures outfitted to withstand water and city designs that support aquatic living. He designs better, with a vision of structural materials that won't degrade easily, rather than the materials used to construct flashy arrangements that seem only to last long enough to attract a few high budget tenants. With each new project, Len hopes that Earth will be more prepared to face the reckoning to come. And with each new project, Len considers himself one of Earth's little Habitable Status soldiers.

Now, ten years later, the day has come for those twenty-four crew members to finally have their feet bound again to Earth's soil. The reckoning Len anticipates creeps ever closer.

Len turns away from the mental image in his head of the anchor and goldfish insignia, turns away from his little sister's bright face in uniform, turns away from the wall in his kitchen where his prized paper calendar hangs, and walks into his living room where his most treasured trove of counsel are gathered in front of his Electronic Assistant-managed television. The assembly of three familiar faces brings peace to Len, even if they do make fun of him for continuing to use tactile items like his precious paper calendar.

Michael Aparna, Doctor of Environmental and Marine Engineering, Vivien Ashen, Doctor of Marine Biology and Geology, and Ren Barge,

Assistant Professor of Artificial Intelligence, garnish the two blue suede couches in Len's living room with their presence. Len invited nearly his entire Civil Engineering Department but is pleased to find the attentive gazes of only Doctor Aparna, Doctor Ashen, and Assistant Professor Barge. Ironically, none of them are actually from his department. Rather, they saw his clipping on the STEM College's Bulletin and took it as their welcome invitation to join. Had there been more bodies than three, Len is certain his modest home would be overflowing just like the oceans. Besides, Len actually knows Michael, Vivien, and Ren on a first name basis. Many of the colleagues in his department insist on actually being called by their formal titles that Len prefers only to attach to them in his head. The doctors casually glance towards Len as he enters the room while talking listlessly amongst themselves.

"Greetings, Len," Deborah, the Electronic Assistant, says from the speakers of the television. "Everyone is speculating that WHP will have news transformative for your profession." One of Len's three visitors coughs suggestively. "And your contemporaries' professions. You all will be quite implicated in the quest to fix Earth."

"Thank you, Deb. I am sure we will be." Len sits down on the arm chair of his blue suede couch. His colleagues' eyes are glued to the live-stream of Florida's Cape Canaveral Space Base, where, way back in '54, the WHP's three spacecraft carrying an aggregate of twenty-four Space Team members first lifted off.

"So what do you think WHP is going to announce at this press conference today? I know the WHP Space Team has been in regular contact with the WHP Ground Team, but their reports and plans haven't really been made public," Ren says.

"That's my understanding too, and you know how much I like scouring the WWW for any scientific research and reports on this topic," Vivien remarks.

"*And you know* how much *I* like scouring the WWW for hot news about how we might manage to prolong humanity's little stint here on Earth," Ren replies. Vivien's cheeks flush and a laugh tries to escape her closed mouth. Vivien's mouth was always closed in thought when she wasn't sharing information or a sassy remark. "I've resigned myself to avidly watching the speculation videos all over Wwick," Ren says.

"I would hazard," says Michael, "that the WHP will break down their action items over the next six months, year, three years. Whatever. They've spent all this time and a huge wad of money on Mission Habitable Status. Bet they've been ironing out all of the plans and going back and forth internally, you know, on what's best and most effective. They owe it to the public now though – we've been patient enough – to disclose exactly what we can expect our government, and all the invested corporations, will do to protect our society from, well, completely ceasing."

Len sits on the arm of the couch Michael occupies and hears the sounds Michael's larynx makes, but he has already begun losing himself in his own thoughts as the livestream of Cape Canaveral and his colleagues drone on. All the news coverage of the crew's return reminds Len of how, prior to launch, WHP almost implemented an all-woman crew.

At the time, some of the more popular space agencies were encouraging an all-woman crew due to what they termed an "increased likelihood of survival." They posited that women, on the whole, exhibit "more compassion, less risk-taking, and less homicidal tendencies."

Automobile Insurance companies used to have insurance policies based on similar concepts, at least before self-driving cars took over the market.

The globe, and more specifically the media giant Wwick, erupted in fury at these space agencies' gendered perspectives. But, even in fury, the people of Earth could not pick a single counter argument. There were many more than one. And it was a whole divisive debacle.

Apparently, some folks thought that sending only women on this quest was actually more dangerous because of something they called "hormonal syncing" as well as a perceived phenomenon of women tearing women down, whether emotionally or physically. This upset a lot of people, even if, and especially when, many of them had experienced the latter.

Then, there were other folks who thought it unfair to discriminate against men. *What did men ever do to women?* Those proponents asked. Len's wife had a long list to answer that. His sister did too.

And those weren't the only disgruntled responses against the woman-only crew concept. Some folks argued that the crew's composition should be merit-based. Pretty much everyone thought that makes plain sense, but still nobody could agree on what qualifies as qualities of excellence. And, some folks who didn't fall into the whole this-discriminates-against-men camp still thought it dangerous not to represent half of society on a quest to save society. But even this didn't really capture all of the disgruntled feelings against the women-only crew concept. There were also folks who protested that society wasn't split into two halves; everyone in between man and woman should be invited based on their merit, and for additional perspective, too. HUMANS EXIST ON A GRAY-SCALE AND NOT ONLY IN BLACK AND WHITE, Len saw written on posters outside the Federal Reserve Bank of Colorado, which was the site of a huge Wake-Up-WHP protest.

At the time, he giggled because black and white compose the gray-scale. Many users took to Wwick to point this out. Len wasn't one of them. He felt the sentiment of the protesters because, he too, was not a simple, two dimensional being. *We live in a grey area*, he agreed.

Needless to say, as a result of the world stage erupting in fury, WHP reconsidered its concept of an all-woman crew. Instead, WHP chose to broaden its request for applicants by excluding identity qualifications from the job description. Applicants need not hold a certain job position, nor identify their educational institutions attended, nor birth order, nor provide their surname in their visible application. The good news: anyone who did anything could now apply to serve in WHP's quest for a habitable Earth.

The CEO of WHP held a press conference on the matter to thank the globe for its influence in developing a qualified team of mixed perspective and ability. "The global market place of ideas pulled through for WHP over the past several months of protests," the CEO proclaimed. "We recognize our original crew concept had room for growth, and we are proud to announce our crew will encompass roles beyond the typical Astronaut for our Inundo mission." And thus, the crew was ultimately composed of scientists, engineers, global security analysts, diplomats, and even a trusty IT guy, too.

Len agreed that WHP would need many different kinds of brains, reactions, and thoughts if Earth wanted out of the box thinking about how oxygen and nitrogen-dependent creatures could survive a much more hydrogen dense environment. Len appreciated that the Earth's heroes of tomorrow were composed of everybody. Humans only took long enough to act in union rather than hold fast to their long-worn patterns of in-group and out-group fighting, which often distracts from the end goal.

Of course, WHP considered many other items aside from the composition of its crew before the '54 liftoff. Many of them were actually much more trivial than who could compose the crew – what color the spacecraft should be, who would be engaged to design and manufacture them, what the crew's insignia should look like, whether they should have a flag and, if so, what color it should be, and so on.

WHP was founded as a private company, although many government leaders held a stake, albeit a minority stake. Many of those government leaders were military and insisted the best color scheme for the spacecraft would be camouflage. Varying shades of blue to mesh with the various colors of water. However, many of WHP's large, private sector investors insisted on red and yellow, which represented several of the largest brands. A few popular conspiracy theorists on Wwick, who owned much of WHP's stock, resisted the government's objective to camouflage the ship in blue because, how can humans trust the government to know the color of the water on another planet? And if the government did know, was it really telling us *everything* it knew? The government is hardly forthright or accurate about the facts of major assassinations. When the color question was put to a vote after almost a year of debate, the board decided that a single shade of royal blue would be best. The board reasoned that red and yellow served no survival function, and camouflage may indicate to Inundans that humans were trying to trick them. Further, the board found cyan blue to be far too light a color to be intimidating and navy blue to be far too dark a color to be friendly.

The companies bidding on WHP contracts were scrutinized by the public. The public proclaimed, "Butteford Mechanics Inc. hardly engages in any eco-investing," and "Ezzquisite Co. hardly closes the wage gap and had that huge insider-trading scandal with coal stock last quarter." The consensus seemed to be that WHP should accept an offer from a company whose practices most aligned with actually creating a habitable Earth. But even the companies doing most of the socially and environmentally responsible work still weren't doing enough. "Freagull Corp hits the mark on its hiring practices, but it's the 2050s now, they should be auto-enrolling their employees in 401k plans with automatic dividend reinvestment in carbon offsetting stock."

The CEO's niece designed the insignia. Nepotism is a tradition too longstanding to completely overturn.

WHP did decide to adopt a mission flag. The Americans took a flag to the Moon, so WHP was determined to bring a global flag to Inundo. But the process of adopting a design was lengthy. Many Countries were amicable to at least a bit of red in the flag; Canada and Greenland were huge supporters of a crisp, red apple color. Jamacia wanted a flag with a huge X through the middle, but the United States pushed back because their people had been through enough with those types of flags. And then Cambodia and Macau began advocating for a flag without stars, which was unpopular at first considering the interstellar nature of the mission but really gained traction when Mexico suggested a flag with a wreath. Ultimately, the WHP board decided that a black flag with a grey overlay image of three olive branches composing a wreath was best. Black and grey are neutral and plants and birds are minimally evocative.

Len supposes now, these considerations may not be so trivial. The color of the spacecraft could certainly impact the crew's survival should survival-by-hiding become necessary. The insignia might offend intelligent life. Not that there were many options on the insignia design part. Len found himself perplexed. Not by the nepotism but by the divides these seemingly trivial matters surfaced and how just one of them single handedly pushed back the launch date by a year. *Are we humans too focused on blaming others and creating little fires to solve our own larger problems? Or do we simply tend to strive in the direction of progress against any and all friction and cost?*

The television streamer interrupts Len's thoughts, and Deborah broadcasts an aerial view of the space base's geometric ground design onto the television. The doctors sitting on the couch by Len watch in silent anticipation. Snapping out of his thoughts, Len notices with mild surprise that there are absolutely zero palm trees on the space base. He knows the lack of palm trees makes sense for a place where rockets launch but notes it makes much less sense for Florida's image on the whole.

His chest deflates as he sighs in relief. Sometimes space bases *are* designed for functionality and not to fit governmental image. Len was so used to the latter being the motivation.

Shore Protector boats fill the television screen. The boats float off the north of the space base prepared to make their retrieval of the WHP Space Team from the spacecraft when they parachute into the Atlantic Ocean. The Shore Protectors' watchful eyes contain a serious look that extends beyond the horizon. That horizon is higher now than it was ten years ago. In seven years, nothing will rise above it.

Michael glances at Len from behind his green framed eyeglasses, eyeglasses two generations newer than Len's, and says, "What do you figure their plan will be, Len?"

"Well, that all depends on the technological advancements they've been able to make in these past six years." Len ponders how much data a crew of twenty-four, not entirely composed of scientists, could gather in two years. He thinks, also, of the modeling a team of thousands could run in four years with such data.

"Yeah, totally. What kind of technological advancements do you think WHP's made? How do you think they'll impact our work?"

"Well, a lot of our limitations in addressing the woes of the world prior to Mission Habitable Status were due to our inability to control the climate. And then, of course, there were some other limitations, too." Len pauses to take in his surroundings. Vivien is sitting at the absolute edge of the couch, her right elbow propped on her knee and right hand cradling her face. Her very serious, tightly lipped, pensive face. Len often found it difficult to know when Vivien was listening intently or silently criticizing. Len continues. "Limitations like our inability to resource large quantities of the raw materials we'd need to build stilted structures or to build nuclear power reactors quickly at a global scale, and also our knowledge, skill, and labor force to do so."

He tries picturing all of New York City on stilts. He tries imagining agriculture without soil. One of those scenarios is much easier for Len to visualize than the other. Afterall, the hydroponic industry continues to grow year over year. But WHP can't save New York City with hydroponics.

Len can sense the marine biologist in Vivien itches to speak to the hazardous effects of nuclear energy and by-products on the environment. But he finishes his thought while she fiddles with one of the rings on her middle finger: "Without those resources and clean, renewable power, we're not only limited in mitigating harmful environmental effects, but we couldn't even build enough spacecraft to transport our global population to a new world, not even Mars. And we've been too fixated on going to Planet B for all these years. As a result, we, number one, cared less about treating Earth well and leaned into comfort and, number two, failed to research planets other than Mars. Now our maltreatment of Earth, hesitation to invest in renewables, and undiversified space research have caught up to us."

"So how do you think it'll impact our work?" Asks Michael again, getting back to the point.

"So I see one of three things happening: either Inundo has taught us to build tools or produce enough clean energy to control the environment and we are brought on to scale clean power supply and design safe cities, or Inundo has given us the blueprints to build a civilization high above the water and we are tasked with implementing stilted city plans, or Inundo has given us the blue prints to build a civilization far below the water and we get contracted to design our own little underwater world."

Michael replies, "We called it, didn't we?" Excitement twinkles in his eyes. Knowing Michael, Len guesses he cannot wait for the seafaring market to expand. Better yet, Michael probably cannot wait for WHP to fund contaminated site remediation on a larger scale.

"You know what we called?" Asks Vivien, rhetorically of course. "That our vastly lacking knowledge of the marine world would certainly come to frighten our future."

Michael blushes at the marine biologist's humor and chuckles his acquiescence. As an expert in environmental and marine engineering himself, he is aware of the knowledge he lacks about what is in the depths of the Earth's oceans. Yet he knew infinitely more about the ocean than the average global citizen. Yet another area of research the world has paid far too little attention: oceanography.

Certainly, everyone in the room has noticed the growing popularity of articles concerning frightful fish from beyond. The *Global Topographers* most recent feature spread regarding increased, unexplained marine disturbances did not do much to assuage the fears of the public. "Unexplained marine disturbances" is how the *Global Topographers* likes referring to the ocean equivalent of unidentified flying objects since the scientific community is hesitant to accept the term unidentified swimming objects. Contrary to popular belief, unidentified swimming objects are about as common as unidentified flying objects and the increase in such sightings is actually explicable by the increase in awareness and reporting of USOs that were formerly occurring but unnoticed. A lot of them really aren't that threatening.

"Well whatever information WHP is able to gather from the civilization of an underwater planet is sure to impact civil engineering and interstellar diplomacy," Len says, clarifying for the doctor of marine biology and geology who so often thinks that the ocean is at the center of everything. Although, Len supposes, she probably is right this time, given the three, five, and seven-year projections the WHP published last week. Every news organization is talking about those projections WHP extrapolated from data routinely gathered about Earth's water levels, temperatures, and gases: Earth's existing continents are expected to completely submerge within seven years.

Len always doubted the success of this WHP mission. He particularly doubted that the globe would ever get to the point it would actually press the button to send a crew off in search of answers. In his experience, the people of Earth are often too distracted or too focused on blaming others to help themselves. The outburst over who was qualified to compose the crew was a perfect example of that. Humans often see nothing but trees in the face of threats that demand they look at the whole forest.

Len tugs on the ends of his collared sleeves like he always does when he's nervous. But he is not nervous for the WHP's findings.

The WHP Space Team sent back formal, routine reports to the WHP Ground Team every quarter summarizing their latest situational (often anthropological and technological) developments. The WHP Space Team confirmed in early '58 that their mission proved fruitful. They found Inundans. Or aquarians. Aquarians is how Len liked to think of them, what with them being all aqua-involved as they are. But the WHP and the media refer to them traditionally as Inundans. Which Len isn't a particular fan of, given the etymology being so closely drawn to "swamp." He did not think of Aquarians as swamp people. They were not ogres after all.

What Len is actually nervous for is what this information means for Earth. *Sure, this information is supposed to ensure humanity's survival. But what will humanity be in a groundless world? In an underwater world? What will reality be? What will we do for fun? And what about our new neighbors?*

The conversation in Len's living room peters out. The television now streams commentary by one of its anchormen:

"The Space Team that WHP composed nearly a decade ago is expected to land here, off the coast of Cape Canaveral, Florida, in the next four hours. It was in 2054 that the WHP deployed this crew of twenty-four brave globe trotters, now space trotters, on a mission to our neighboring water-giant, Inundo. Factoring in travel time, the WHP Space Team has had only two years of research and development on Inundo. However, we understand that the Space Team has worked relentlessly in partnership with the Ground Team here on Earth to concoct a plan to return our globe to Habitable Status. We await their return and WHP's anticipated formal announcement and plan to deliver global humanitarian aid and infrastructure redevelopment. Anni, back to you."

The camera pans to a woman's face as she sits behind a large mahogany desk. Her lips are thin and tightly pursed. Her eyes are either a bit sunken into her face by nature or she hasn't gotten enough sleep in the last five days. Len remembers seeing her on several nightly talk shows in the past decade hosting political debates about the best way to integrate humanity into a sunken world. "Just ask Venice!" was one of her quirkier remarks in the early days. She must be tired of joking by now.

"You know, I cannot believe that the time period of two years is sufficient for gathering effective data and tools to aid our situation here," says Vivien. "I get that the WHP has to balance the time sensitivity of the world ending against the timetable for scientific invention and perfection of methods," Vivien sighs, "but that's just ridiculous." Vivien sits next to Michael on the couch and slouches over with her head in her hands. Michael glances at her and, after several moments of consideration, pats her back gently in consolation.

"Vivien, you forget that the WHP team in space has been working jointly with the WHP team here on Earth. This is part of why I love

Wwick. They build up my confidence in the mission and our survival prospects so much. Wwick's streamers give video updates about the cool new technologies they speculate WHP is working on. And all the best software companies are working with the WHP these days. The optics help their shareholder engagement anyway, even if the public's still in the dark about the actual solutions developed," says Ren. Len smiles. Len likes when Ren puts all the doctors in their place.

"Ren's got a point, Vivien," Len says, affirming his support. "That would put the total time for WHP's research and development at six years. Plus, our past generations knew the speed with which Pear Software developed touchless mobiles – Generation 31 came out the same year as Generation 20 – it was ridiculous. Now we are harnessing that same efficiency of the private market for the public good. And it just might save us."

Anni's face remains on the large, flatscreen in front of them. Her lips finally part from their solemn stance as she speaks. "Thanks, Brad. Listeners, stay tuned. We'll be back with updates as the hours progress." The streaming service cut to commercial break – that being a streaming takeover by no other than sustainability influencer Jessica Becker. Len thought to himself, *How appropriate.* Granted, there was no shortage of sustainability influencers these days. Almost every other commercial stream featured one.

"Well," says Ren as he points to Len's patio door, "I don't know about you, but I am ravenous and the EatMeet you have smoking out there smells delicious." Len had left the door open with the screen closed so his nose could clock the EatMeet's cook time.

"Be my guest," says Len. He checks his watch to confirm and then says, "it should be just about ready."

"Hopefully the news they have for us later doesn't make us sick," says Viven. "I'd rather not taste your infamous EatMeet more than once."

"Hey, Viv," says Ren in an ironically chipper tone, "that's a much more positive take than imagining the WHP announcement might imply this is our last supper."

~

The year is 2058 and Special Agent May Rivers is suspended in orbit around Inundo. She is about to radio General Inglett to discuss new information pertinent to Mission Habitable Status.

The WHP Space Team arrived two weeks ago. One of the three spacecraft already fell into Inundo's waters. Rivers would be on the last of the three spacecraft to break Inundo's orbit and plunge into its depth. For two weeks, Rivers and the crew on her spacecraft have been monitoring the first team from orbit.

The Space Team decided to stagger their exploration of Inundo – introducing one spacecraft at a time to best ensure the success of their quest. The first spacecraft to break orbit was, in Rivers' mind, the bravest. They knew not what lay below. They knew not whether they would survive. Of course, they had a pretty good idea that they would. WHP retrofitted their spacecraft to accommodate oceanic travel such that each vessel was more akin to an amphibious vessel: equipped to be submarines almost as much as they were equipped to be spacecraft. But the crew still didn't know for a fact whether all WHP's preparation would pay off.

While the spacecraft could act as submarines, once they became such, it wasn't entirely clear whether the acting submarines could again become spaceborne – what with the whole flying-out-of-water thing. WHP prepared the crew as much as possible based on the math – how long each leg of the trip would be (158,550 AU), how much food supply would be necessary, how reliable their already orbiting satellites would be for their communications systems, how takeoff and landing should work. But they hadn't been able to test some of their systems outside of theory. Liftoff from Inundo, for instance, was a question mark. The Ground Team advised them that submerged liftoff was possible, although many of the mechanisms would depend on the atmosphere, pressure, and structure of wherever they landed. WHP estimated Inundo's surface gravitational force through known variables and estimated the proper acceleration and pitch needed for successful liftoff; however, estimates are still not actuals. So they would just need to try and see.

When the first-wave team first broke orbit and dove into Inundo, they were able to ascertain those variables. But those variables weren't the only information WHP needed. They needed news of positive diplomatic engagement with the lifeforms WHP observed from unmanned missions. Then, they needed a whole lot more information from those lifeforms *if* they decided to cooperate. Like how they survive underwater. Hopefully, the information could lead Earth to adopt similar practices.

~

Commander Zibowitz led the first-wave team into the waters below. Commander Heretzel would do so next. And Commander Rivers would lead the final team. When Zibowitz's spacecraft splashed down, he let the then-submarine surface so he could radio in using the satellites WHP stationed around Inundo years ago. Static overlay the first-wave commander's voice: "We've landed. Our vessel is in-tact. Two crew members are a bit sick, but we are all alive. We'll take the measurements requested of us by Ground Team. Then, our first objective is to detect life. Ideally, we can locate a colony of the lifeforms or a whole civilization if we're really lucky," reported Commander Zibowitz. Their first good news.

"Copy, Zibowitz. Continue pursuing your first objective and break the surface to check in with us on a 24-hour cycle. We will take no contact to mean mishap," responded Commander Heretzel.

"Roger."

Their second good news came 78 hours later. This time it came from Ground Team. They received the data pushed through by the Zibowitz's team and were modeling solutions for submerged liftoffs. "It's looking good, Commanders. Of course, be sure Zibowitz's team monitors these measurements daily. We're not familiar with the inner workings of Inundo and don't know what could change or how rapidly."

Zibowit'z team checked in every 24 hours. By hour 144, or day 6, Zibowitz's team observed 4 instances of USOs. A few crew members sighted rippling water due to external object movement and another crew member detected a wide range of sound velocities indicating objects both small and large nearby using the spacecraft's sonar abilities. That crew member quickly shared this happenstance with absolutely everyone on board. To be fair, everyone on board agreed it was, indeed, exciting news.

"So what's it like?" Rivers asked Zibowitz on an inter-wave Commanders call one week into their field work on Inundo.

"Really, very teal."

"Have you seen life yet?"

"Not yet. But WHP is certain it's out here. And so am I and the crew on board."

About two weeks after deploying the first wave crew to conduct field work, the Space Team received orders from the Ground Team to deploy the second wave upon sight of life. The Ground Team's monitoring had confirmed the variables measured were stable, and the team had confidence in their submerged liftoff concept. Ongoing monitoring by Heretzel's and Rivers' second and third-wave teams conducted from orbit indicated there were electrical signals beneath the water-covered planet. They hoped this meant life. And not just the life the Space Team deployed itself. In fact, WHP measured the electrical signals on Inundo before commencing Mission Habitable Status. And the electrical signals Space Team picked up from orbit reflected two different rates of electrical impulses, perhaps indicating two types of life.

Not two days later than the Space Team received their orders to deploy the second wave upon sight of life, life was sighted. Hernandez, the crew member monitoring the spacecraft's sonar, called Zibowitz over. Hernandez was shocked to discover, first by sonar and then by visual, that a small submarine lay no more than 100 feet before them. "Zibowitz! Get yourself over here! I have Inundans at one o'clock!" Hernandez pointed to a sizable red blob in the lower right side of the navigation screen.

Zibowitz's jaw dropped. "Can we send some extremely low frequency signals?"

"How do we know they won't torpedo us, Sir? Or their technological equivalent of it?"

"They would have done that already, Hernandez. We don't provoke them; they won't provoke us."

"Okay, Sir. ELF it is." Hernandez leaned forward, toggled a few buttons and knobs, and sat back to wait while a low pitch traveled out from their spacecraft. Both he and Zibowitz trained their eyes on the submarine lurking beyond the thick window. Silence ensued. But not for long. A low pitch, created without their spacecraft, traveled toward them. "Sir! We've made contact!" Herandez fidgeted excitedly in his chair and turned toward Zibowitz for direction. But something had caught Zibowitz's eye.

"Hernandez, what do you make of –" Zibowitz hunched over and pointed to the sonar navigation screen, where a smaller red blob had broken away from the initial red blob and was moving toward them.

"Are they sending one of theirs?"

Zibowitz stood straight, as if doing so would gather his thoughts. "I'll gather the crew. We may need to send one of our diplomats soon." He left the compartment and returned moments later with an eager swath of scientists and the first-wave team's diplomat and language specialist, Ngo. The smaller red blob on the sonar navigation screen was already much closer. "Team, we have a visual of an Inundan submarine. In fact, we have visual of an Inundan approaching our spacecraft. So far, our interaction has been peaceful. I want us prepared. It's go-time." Zibowitz nodded to Specialist Ngo, who turned to gather scuba equipment.

And now Rivers is here on a call with the General. "As our data foresaw, there's life on Inundo."

"Well tell me more, Rivers," commands the General.

"The life on Inundo is intelligent. From Zibowitz's description of the specimen he saw, they are bi-pedal like we are; although their feet are larger on average and webbed. They have arms and eyes quite similar to ours, and perhaps more notably, a respiratory system more like ours than like fish," Rivers reports. The General sits straighter in her chair. She looks at Rivers in a way that could be confused with hope.

"So how exactly do they respire underwater? Or do we know whether they remain underwater? Do they have some technology enabling them to enclose their shelter in a breathable bubble? Or perhaps they use breathing apparatuses?" The General's eyebrows thread together as she waits to digest more of Rivers' words.

Rivers explains to General Inglett the Space Team's preliminary understanding of how Inundans live. "They live underwater in shelters tucked away into coral reefs that are constructed as sort of oxygenariums, like the bubble idea you mention, and they respire outside of those structures through parasites." The general's face looked to be a mixture of bewilderment and disgust. "You know, one of those parasites that's mutually beneficial to both the host and the parasite. I forget the Latin term." The general nods. She is aware of such organisms, although not first-hand. "Their underwater biome appears to be quite complex upon a glance at our first dataset."

"So where exactly do the parasites attach to their host?" Asks the general. Rivers pauses before responding.

"Their face." Rivers replies.

The general nods. "And their hosts do not suffocate or experience any other notable, detrimental effects?"

"No, rather the contrary. The parasites are oxygen-producing and carbon dioxide consuming in just about the perfect quantities for both Inundan and human respiration. We each require about the same level of oxygen the parasites produce and exhale about the same level of carbon dioxide the parasites require for sustenance."

"And we have measured this, surely? The gaseous quantities emitted and required by the parasites and the Inundans? We know, factually, that we are comparable?"

"Of course, General. Our Space Team scientists have measured many times over since our first contact and the results are consistent. We're pleased the Inundans have, so far and so quickly, been rather cooperative."

"I would say I wonder how a world so brimming with water has mammals within it who breathe so much like us." General Inglett remarks. "But then, I suppose, our own world is full of seals, whales, and dolphins." She pauses. Many thoughts seem to move over her face at once. "You would think, perhaps, they wouldn't have survived."

"Well, news of mammals who, as unlikely as it seems, survive such an environment is rather hopeful for our own fate," adds Rivers. "Better even that mammals have already gone before where we soon will on our own planet."

~

Several months have passed since Zibowitz's team made first contact with the Inundans, although the humans' total time on Inundo is just under a year.

"Acquirians," mumbles Jeji from her plush, velvet-like seat in the convening room. Jeiji is one of seven Inundans appointed for life to govern the inhabitants of Inundo. She and the rest of the seven governors of Inundo have been in diplomatic discussions with the Earthen for the past twenty-six moons.

"These Acquirians force our panel into growing pains. Learning to live with their presence and respond to their every nosy request about how we live is thoroughly tedious. I do predict they shall plague us." Her right leg lays daintily over her left, but she kicks it off, readjusting her posture to better communicate her dissatisfaction with her government's current arrangement. An anklet created from material resembling Abalone shells clinks slightly from the movement as it comes to rest against the cyan blue ankles connected to Jeiji's size 13, webbed feet.

"Halt your pessimism, Jeji," Fion interjects turning to face Jeiji in the seat beside hers. Fion sat in on almost all of the initial meetings with the Earthen. Before Inundans and the Earthen could communicate verbally, she was drawn to their measured approach, curiosity, and use of nonverbal cues. They seemed alert, but not hostile. She doesn't think the Earthen are the threat Jeiji thinks they are.

"I tell you, Fion," responds Jeiji, "the aptitude for these creatures to acquire the next best thing and forget all that the old ways ever did for them is absolutely unparallelled. Have you listened when they explain why their planetary sphere is in this predicament?"

Fion rolls her eyes and turns to the trident beside her with her back toward Jeiji. She heard the story herself from the Earthen dispatched from their strangely shaped ship. The story goes that, long ago, the Earthen discovered how to produce products and use scarce resources and realized far too recently exactly how monstrous those activities were to their Earth. But Fion found their hope charming and was quite swayed by their offerings to share their self-developed technologies with Inundo. Inundans crave knowledge.

Fion replies, "Perhaps, but you frame it as though they only take," and runs her deep indigo index finger along the length of her trident. Her purple eyes widen in mild frustration and the light refracting through the transparent ceiling of the convening room glints briefly off them. "And is not their desire to revive their Earth a display of wanting to keep the old rather than acquire a new planetary sphere?" Jeiji huffs. Fion considers Jeiji's exasperation as a concession.

"The diva has a point," chimes in Seeink, Chair of the Inundan Governing Panel, referring to Jeiji. Seeink continues, "I find it quite baffling that the Earthen claim they could not lessen the harm to their planetary sphere. With all their self-made technologies, you would think they could have developed functional nuclear energy by now. And while they have come close, they simply haven't found it economical to do so.

Do you, fellow governors, find it reasonable to trust beings that cannot find the value in investing in their own preservation? Would they care if what they ask of us risks *our* preservation? I can hardly imagine they would be more sensitive to the survival of others than to the survival of themselves."

Each member of the governing panel grunts their consideration and disfavor of this thought. They sit still in their velvet adorned chairs behind the large O-shaped table before them, contemplating Seeink's words and perhaps their own impressions of the Earthen. Some members fiddle with their tridents as his words seep in.

"Catre would like to make a point," Catre says. "Catre agrees with Seeink and Jeiji on the basis that these beings had many opportunities to help themselves. Their own egos interfered to their species' detriment. They confessed it themselves when informing us of their global accords. Recall how the leaders of their whole planetary sphere would meet to set benchmarks and design plans to lower some of these Carbon Emissions they speak of, which would have saved them from their present doom. Also recall how every leader wanted the outcome but few of them, especially those most capable of payment, wanted to foot the bill."

"Baffling," comments Seeink.

Sealy breaks into the conversation from her perch in the corner of the convening room, "But, to Fion's point, the Earthen bring great discoveries to us."

Skepticism is written across Seeink's face as he regards Sealy. His teal ears wiggle, and his nose scrunches at the bridge between his eyes.

Sealy says, "Think of their description of threading cables across our planet's floor and enabling communication amongst our inhabitants by connection to what they call a Single Network. Sure, they have not achieved the *same* technological abilities as us. As Seeink pointed out, their use of nuclear energy is still rather novice, but that does not make them *below* us, it only makes them *different* than us. Their way of living did not necessitate the technologies our way of living does. They give us what tools they do have, and we take those tools eagerly. Perhaps some of us do so out of pride to boast about just how much better our tools are than theirs, but we hesitate to acknowledge that those tools actually *can* advance our resources." Sealy looks content with her speech. Receiving silence from the governing panel, she looks from Seeink to Jeiji. "Look, you two, all I am saying is that we have the same propensity to acquire as do they."

Jeiji sighs exasperatedly again and plays with a trinket draped around her wrist made from the same material as her anklet. Everyone in the room understands this is Jeiji's body language for, "I'm not convinced."

"We merely acquire knowledge," Jeiji bites, "while *they* acquire limited resources and use them too quicky and have to acquire *more* limited resources."

Silence takes the room again. "Our species acquires knowledge, but we also covet influence. And we are positioned perfectly to acquire a seat on an interplanetary stage," adds Fion. Fion is surprised the governing panel is not brimming with enthusiasm and pride. They are so close to reaching a deal with the Earthen to acquire voting rights, immigration, and visiting rights to their Earth.

But Fion supposes the rest of the governing panel is less than enthused. *Why would they want access to a planetary sphere that was dying? And, why does Fion think access would benefit them anyway?*

Perhaps, Fion considers, her generation feels differently about exploring above the surface of Inundo than the elder generations do. The tradition of Inundo is to thoroughly understand their surroundings. To innovate their everyday lives and look deeper *within* their world – not farther away. But Fion was elected to her lifetime appointment by the younger generation and feels a sense of duty to see their new ideal of outward discovery through. Afterall, might outward discovery lead to inward insight?

Jeiji's voice interrupts Fion's thoughts. "They call us Swamp people for Jove's sake, Fion, and they sought us out to receive more from us than they intended to give. And they prefer to blame at a higher frequency than they prefer to act for themselves. I could go on." Jeiji's protest draws attention from all of the members of the governing panel, who wobble their heads from side to side as though ensuring their brain matter weighs both sides of the argument.

Fion reads the body language of everyone in the convening room. Catre, Seeink, and Stephen rally behind Jeiji, slinking looks her way and positioning their feet toward her chair and away from Fion's. Sealy and Sicile, like Fion, are steady in their view that the Earthen offer value to their people. The room is just about split in how they feel toward the Earthen. Fion needs to persuade just one of the governor's on Jeiji's side before the panel's vote.

"Is it fair to say, fellow panel members, that we are giving an incredible increment of time and knowledge to the Earthen when we agree to advise them on survival below what they term Water?" Fion looks around the room and sees many teal and indigo heads nod. "I agree, my fellow governors." Fion sits a little straighter, with her shoulder blades pulled back and confidence rising. "We must choose wisely what we do with our and our inhabitants' time. I acknowledge your concerns."

The panel members sit still, and their heads only move slightly with a gentle interest in Fion's words. Fion speaks again: "Please allow me to remind you that Inundan society is based upon the foundational beliefs in loyalty and knowledge. Are not the humans looking to continue their residency on their Earth? Is not that a display of loyalty? They are not seeking a new world; their plan excludes the acquisition of some shiny new planetary sphere. We know they do not come here for that. Instead, they come here for knowledge to see through their loyalty to Earth. What is more Inundan than that?"

Now the panel members shift their gaze to the archway windows lining the convening room. Fion interprets their away-gaze as deep thought rather than an offense. It is common courtesy in Inundan society to allow each other personal space to think without the immediate reaction of others clouding one's judgment.

Fion wants to thicken her point still. "Might we potentially benefit from a vote on an interplanetary stage? Might we desire influence on a larger scale?" She allows a few moments for this to sink in and then poses a final question. "Don't we owe it to our people to entertain an idea like this, even if, ultimately, we decide against it? Let us give it time to rest in our minds before deciding. Chair Seeink, may we reconvene in two weeks' time?"

"Yes, fellow governor," Chair Seeink replies, "we shall reconvene in two weeks' time." He picks up the trident in his lap and taps it against the palm of his teal hands. "Adjourned."

~

Two weeks have passed since the Inundan Governing Panel's last debate regarding Inundan-Earthen relations. Fluid pricks Fion's skin. She wouldn't sweat in the currents of the sea and wishes now she could leave the confines of the convening room to go for a brief swim.

She reflected after the last governing panel meeting about how her fellow governors see the world so differently than she. Quickly, she realized, she was making the wrong appeal. She had been asking her society to think about the similarities between their own ideals and a society completely outside of themselves that they knew little about. She had been implying to an *interior*-focused nation they might want *external* influence. She needed to show them what the Earthen value. She needed to reflect how external influence was an asset to their domestic policy and how, not to pursue such influence, could hurt their adored homeland.

The governing panel of Inundo now funnels into the convening room. The panel is to meet today to discuss whether they shall enter a diplomatic agreement with the Earthen. Fion settles into her throne-like chair and pulls her shoulders down and back against the chair. She must lead with confidence if there is any more convincing to be done. They are to announce their decision with their inhabitants at large as soon as their discussion concludes.

Seeink looks from governor to governor from behind the large O-shaped table before him. The governors settle into their seats and return eye contact with Seeink who then opens the floor to discussion. "We converse today about whether to enter into contract with the Earthen and, if so, what our obligations and the Earthen's obligations shall be."

Jeiji is the first to pound the table. Her trident whacks the tabletop with a loud thud. "I think it not in the best interest of our inhabitants to proceed with any contract other than one of isolationism." Fion feels disappointment cloud her vision. She nearly misses Stephen raising his navy, webbed hand to object.

"Now, I have contemplated what Fion proposed at our last meeting and, while I understand your view, Jeiji, I think an isolationist policy with the Earthen would be a grave mistake for the wellbeing of our inhabitants."

"Please back up why you think such things, Stephen," Jeiji practically scoffs.

"Gladly." Stephen scoots his chair away from the table and stands. Stephen's frame is unusually large for an Inundan, and his voice holds a certain gravitas at his height. "Fion asked what is more Inundan than the Earthen seeking knowledge to save their planet in an act of loyalty. The only thing of which I can imagine that is more Inundan than that is *Iundans* seeking knowledge to save their planet in an act of loyalty – "

"- But we do not need to save our planet. Our planet is not in jeopardy," says Jeiji.

"Our planet is not in jeopardy *now*, Jeiji. But as cautious leaders, considering that our planet may one day need saving is imperative. In fact, I see two issues with an isolationist policy.

The first is that we cut off an entire realm of awareness prematurely. Sure, we may not think we need to know much about what is beyond our surface. How could it help what lays below? What lays below is most important. Yet, what is beyond our surface may well affect all we consider dear below it. Now, we have some of the best minds, but even our best minds sometimes encounter problems. We Inundans think of problems in a routine way because routine systems usually solve problems best. But sometimes even those systems do not work. We cut ourselves off from thinking differently and to the knowledge that other beings already gathered when we choose isolation. We condemn ourselves to solving our problems alone. And we are, admittedly, a hardworking and independent species. But even we, governors, know one governor cannot solve every problem alone. We know the value of collaboration try as we might to ignore it.

The second is that in failing to learn information and engage in matters external to our world, we fail to prevent our inhabitants from potential harm, which is quite plainly the governing panel's responsibility. I can only speak for myself, but I want to fulfil my responsibilities as a governor."

"Catre would like to argue that, as you say, routine systems solve problems best," says Catre. "Fion even admitted when we last convened that loyalty is one of our species' foundational beliefs. I believe this loyalty extends to knowledge. We prefer tradition. We prefer to build upon our *own* theories. Our *own* science. Formulated by our *own* inhabitants."

"While I am inclined to agree with you, Catre," says Stephen, "researchers heavily compose our population. Many of our brightest theoretical minds are like to view this as an opportunity to test theories and uncover new scientific concepts. Imagine their delight to find out two planetary spheres may hold two different surface gravitational forces. Or enthusiasm to observe the characteristic differences between marine animals on Inundo versus those on Earth. Or to experience new physics, such as those rollercoasters the Earthen are always saying have incredible potential energy."

"See, Stephen, that's precisely the issue," whines Jeiji. "*New* scientific concepts. Inundans care far more for tradition and slowly expanding old thought than diving into new concepts our people had no hand in developing." Her statement brings to the governing panel's mind the six cases of wrongful death at the Downstream School of Sciences the past year. Four professors and two laboratory assistants died in experiments that sought to identify neutrinos and deviated too far from traditional experimental models.

"Jeiji, I will not make light of the tragedy of which I know we are all thinking." Stephen remains standing. He places the trident he has been holding in his left hand gently upon the table. His presence is commanding and somber. "Risk lives in the space between what we know and what we aren't aware of. But, were we to open our eyes, becoming aware may transform us. We have brave researchers on our planet and they willingly confront risk when they seek awareness. They accept risk so willingly because they know their peers may benefit from what they uncover. And in those disasters that we all have in mind, those researchers did uncover new information. Useful information. We find ourselves standing in similar roles now. Risk exists between our tradition and what we aren't aware of. We must accept the risk so our people can benefit from what we uncover."

Fion's throat is cold. She has been listening to her fellow governors speak, not saying a word. And to hear Stephen express his support for a treaty with the Earthen secures her speechlessness.

The convening room is quiet, and the members of the governing panel all avert their eyes from one another in respectful thought. Several minutes pass.

Seeink breaks the quiet with a question to the panel. "Have we any more thoughts?" He allows seven second to pass, looking from member to member, providing time for minds to change or thoughts to come rushing in. None do. "Are we ready for a vote?" Six blue and teal heads nod up and down in unison. "All in favor of an isolationist treaty with the Earthen?" One trident rises from the table. "All in favor of a non-isolationist treaty with the Earthen?" Five tridents raise. "Be it so resolved. We shall enter this treaty as Fion so pled," says Seeink. "Now onto the matters of our obligations and theirs."

~

Rivers, Zibowitz, and Heretzel convene in the third wave ship to discuss the Space Team's return to Earth. On a large monitor in front of them is General Inglett.

"Hello Commanders," the General remarks. "Our two-year period of research and development is almost over. We must work out our strategy for returning the Space Team to Earth." The Commanders nod in unison.

"Rivers, I understand our diplomats report directly to you and, as such, you always seem to have the latest on our relationship with the Inundans."

Rivers nods, "Yes, General."

"Good. I am under the impression the Inundans have no new requests from those set forth in our treaty, correct?"

"Correct, General. The Inundans' requests are still as set forth in our treaty. They provide us with information regarding their survival underwater as well as their technology, and we provide them with Interplanetary Council voting rights, immigration and visiting rights, and shall bring three Inundans with us to Earth on our homebound trip."

The General nods with a self-satisfied look. "Good, Rivers." Heretzel and Zibowitz glance at Rivers hesitantly. The three discussed amongst themselves and the Space Crew the terms of the treaty when it was first made. Neither Heretzel nor Zibowitz thought the terms would be widely accepted by the people of Earth. Rivers felt that whatever terms they could strike with the Inundans that would lead the people of Earth closer to survival would be well worth it. If humans one day decided to critique the WHP's terms of treaty with the Inundans, that at least meant the WHP had bought their survival for another day.

"Rivers, when the Space Team lands at Cape Canaveral, I would like you to speak to our dealing with the Inundans at the press conference. We will need to find an opportune time to introduce the three Inundans who will land with the crew, but I believe a verbal summary would do well before we share our new interplanetary allies in real time."

Rivers shivers at the thought of standing in front of cameras and incessantly curious journalists sharing this news. But she knows it is her job. "Acknowledged, General." Rivers thinks to herself, *I hope they don't shoot the messenger.*

~

"And we're back with a forty-minute countdown to landing," Anni projects her voice through the flatscreen. "Brad, take us through the WHP's agenda from this minute forward." The screen cuts to Brad.

"Thank you, Anni," says Brad. He's still in Cape Canaveral, no palm trees in sight, and his hair is messier than before due to the howling wind. Sun falls on his face as he brushes some of his hair fervently away from his forehead. He's a little sweaty, despite the wind, and wipes his palms on his trousers.

"It's now 15:00 here in Cape Canaveral. Now, beyond our eyesight, the crew aboard the spacecraft has been slowing the spacecrafts' orbital speed and lowering its perigee.

At approximately 15:05, we should be able to see the spacecraft reenter Earth's atmosphere. The sight of the spacecraft may look like warm smudges across the sky to the naked eye. The crew on the spacecraft will be strapped into their seats and maneuvering the controls to continue descent safely.

At approximately 15:25, the ground control here will radio in to the spacecraft and confirm the spacecrafts' planned trajectory. Ground control will be responsible for coordinating with our Shore Protectors here," Brad gestures to the horizon where very official looking folks mill about boats floating on the water, "and the Shore Protector team will later be responsible for water retrieval.

At approximately 15:27, the spacecrafts' parachutes will deploy and ground control will continue to monitor the descent and radio over to the crew on board as to whether the descent remains on target.

From there, we can expect around 15:35 that the spacecraft will be a few hundred feet above sea level.

We're expecting visual confirmation of the splashdown to occur around 15:40." The camera remains focused on Brad as he squints through the Sun's glare bouncing off the camera lens.

"Now, Brad, many citizens are eager for the press conference scheduled following the sea landing. Do we know what to expect from that?" Anni asks on behalf of literally everyone listening to the stream.

~

"We are receiving confirmation that the Space Team has splashed down. The crew that returned from Inundo has held in place to allow hazardous gases to cool off and now the Shore Protectors are retrieving the crew members and bringing them to land trip by trip," Brad reports. The video stream cuts from a landscape scene of the Space Base to a crisp close up of the Atlantic Ocean sloshing up against Shore Protector boats. Three large, royal blue vessels bob in the water.

Len, Michael, Vivien, and Ren watch in anticipation from Len's living room as some of the uniformed Space Team crew step off a Shore Protector boat and onto a dock on the Florida shoreline. The crew members begin to unzip their jumpsuits so as not to overheat, removing their fishbowl helmets and replacing them with hats embroidered with the Mission Habitable Status insignia. A few crew members wipe sweat away from their foreheads. A few stare out at the vast ocean, perhaps contemplating what the depths of their waters will look like after having seen the depths of Inundo.

The video stream focuses in on the most recently collected crew members. Len sits a bit straighter, pulling himself to the edge of the couch cushion underneath him. He sees a face he hasn't seen for ten years – his younger sister May. The set of her jaw and the curls in her hair look so familiar to him, yet her eyes hold a focus more pensive than he remembered. He sees the woman in front of him on the screen and realizes, though he may not have been around to witness it, his little sister has grown up.

She and two other crew members step aside from the group and walk off camera. The stream lingers on the group standing at the dock and the coming and going of the boats collecting and unloading more crew members.

"You have to appreciate that the streaming station is letting us watch so much dead air. Seeing all of this unloading is almost like taking a moment of silence," Ren says. Vivien shoots him a puncturing look. Ren rolls his eyes and makes a zipping gesture across his lips. *Okay. Silence.*

The stream cuts to Brad again. He's standing on a raised platform next to General Inglett and Commanders Zibowitz, Heretzel, and Rivers. "General," Brad says, "We stand here today with you, one of WHP's Ground Team leaders, and the three commanders of WHP's Space Team after all twenty-four Mission Habitable Status crew members have

splashed down on Earth after ten years of travel and research in space."
General Inglett stands with her hands behind her back, right hand grasping her left wrist, posture straight and legs hip-width distance apart. She looks out into the cameras and nods. "The public knows very little about the plans WHP crafted based on the Space Team's findings, and we are all anxious to hear from you today." The General nods again and accepts the old-school handheld microphone Brad hands to her. Streaming stations these days still liked to exude a retro presence.

"Of course. WHP appreciates the public's patience while we work in private to develop a feasible response to the ongoing, global environmental crisis." She turns toward the commanders and says, "Commanders Zibowitz, Heretzel, and Rivers here led a brave mission on a world we formerly had only seen and measured from a distance." Brad looks from commander to commander and his eyes widen as if in realization of how much wider their view of the universe must be than his having been a native Florida streamer all his adult life. "I'll give my voice to them to share the story." General Inglett hands the microphone over to Zibowitz, who clumsily holds it between his two hands.

"The spacecraft I commanded was the first of our three spacecraft to splashdown on Inundo. The water there is incredibly vast and about two weeks passed before we first encountered Inundans." Sweat beads out from under Zibowitz's hat and down the side of his face. "Our diplomat, who's also a language expert, quickly worked with our scientists to establish a communication system with the Inundans, and in time, we were able to converse and share at length about our worlds." Zibowitz turns to Heretzel, ready to pass off the microphone and wipe away his sweat.

"Hi, folks at home," Heretzel says as she manages to wave after accepting the microphone from Zibowitz. "You'll be glad to know that, to add to the story my colleague has laid out, once we were able to communicate verbally as well as nonverbally with the Inundans, we managed to make several scientific breakthroughs. I managed the team of scientists who relentlessly asked questions, measured data, and developed our response to this crisis we knew you were all still facing at home." Heretzel gazes out beyond the cameras trained on her. "I realize, now, we are putting all of our work into action." She glances at Rivers, her eyebrows coming together in a quick motion acknowledging their partnership. "And as we do so," Heretzel looks back out into the sea of cameras, "we need all of your support to save ourselves." Rivers exhales. Her comments come next.

And already Heretzel is passing the microphone off to Rivers, gently squeezing Rivers' hand in support before she lets go.

"Our neighbors, the Inundans, chose to aid us," says Rivers. She feels her voice shake and exhales again, hoping to steady it. "In our time of, admittedly self-inflicted, crisis, a people who did not even know us gave us a second chance to help ourselves." Faces stare at Rivers as she speaks. Each face is patient and nobody seems to breathe. Although, Rivers guesses she could be projecting the last part. "Our diplomatic talks with the Inundans resulted in allyship. You have probably all heard news of our treaty, although I expect the substance of our treaty was held back from you." From his seat at home, Len's chest swells to know his sister was part of orchestrating cordial discussions with the first alien life with which humans have come in contact. He watches intently as she speaks. "We are pleased to share with you today that our neighbors have generously agreed to not only share their rather advanced technologies with us but have also agreed to sponsor, in part, the various retrofitting projects we must undertake to survive beyond seven years. They plan to contribute raw materials from Inundo and other items of value to enable our success." Len's mouth gapes; he doubts humans would have been so generous were situations reversed.

"Our world is indebted to Inundans for this act of grace. Were it not for them, nor for the incredible utility of the biome on their world, we would be counting down our last days." Rivers now gestures to the ocean where the Space Team, only minutes ago, splashed down. "We have invited three of our close Inundan advisors here today to express our thanks. Please receive them with kindness." Rivers feels a gaze on the back of her neck and turns to find General Inglett's piercing eyes on hers. She didn't reveal the immigration plan. She didn't reveal the parasites. But she knew the people of Earth, and she didn't want to incite fear before she could inspire hope.

The journalists in the crowd begin whispering to each other, while the scientists' eyes grow wide. Three Inundans, unfamiliar with Earth's gravity, stumble from the dock toward the platform, guided by a Space Team crew member. They are about to meet their neighbors.

ABOUT THE AUTHOR

Leigh Maris is foremost a reader of cereal boxes, product labels, and tables of contents. Secondarily, she is an author of short musings and forthcoming novels and hopes her words matter to at least one other person. She obtained her Bachelor's of Arts in English Rhetoric and Composition from California State University, Long Beach, where her favorite past time was bringing textbooks to the beach and drinking copious amounts of that coffee that's mainly milk. To support Leigh is also to support the small, terribly cute border collie mix living with her, and most importantly, your own word devouring-habit.

www.ingramcontent.com/pod-product-compliance
Lightning Source LLC
Chambersburg PA
CBHW071216300726
48975CB00004B/1324